W9-DDJ-467

WITHDRAWN

If My Dad Were an Animal

by
Jedda Robaard

little bee books

For Papa with love.

- J.R.

little bee books

An imprint of Bonnier Publishing Group

853 Broadway, New York, New York 10003

Copyright © 2014 by Jedda Robaard. This little bee books edition 2015.

All rights reserved, including the right of reproduction in whole or in part in any form.
LITTLE BEE BOOKS is a trademark of Bonnier Publishing Group, and associated
colophon is a trademark of Bonnier Publishing Group.

Manufactured in China 1014 HH

First Edition 2 4 6 8 10 9 7 5 3 1

Library of Congress Control Number: 2014943627

ISBN 978-1-4998-0036-4

www.littlebeebooks.com
www.bonnierpublishing.com

If my dad were an animal,
he would be a great, big, hairy . . .

yak

If my dad were an animal,
he would be a sleepy, snoozy . . .

koala

If my dad were an animal,
he would surely be a sneaky . . .

monkey

If my dad were an animal,
he would make the perfect stylish . . .

penguin

If my dad were an animal,
he would be a wise, hooty . . .

owl

If my dad were an animal,
he would be a very tall . . .

giraffe

If my dad were an animal,
he would be a strong, burly . . .

elephant

If my dad were an animal,
he would be a big, cuddly . . .

bear!

Because he gives me the best hugs.